C0-AUF-718

THE REAL

HAPPILY EVER AFTER BOOK

SCHOOL OF EDUCATION
CURRICULUM LABORATORY
UM-DEARBORN

21 FAVORITE FAIRY TALES

Simple Narrations
with
Puppets, Masks, and Other Cut-and-Paste Activities
for Young Children

ACKNOWLEDGMENT

The original manuscript of The REAL Happily Ever After Book was edited
and illustrated by Claudia Blamer Breznau.

Special acknowledgment is accorded to Mary Hamilton, whose artistic
flair, and Elaine Raphael, whose careful editing, contributed greatly
to the work in its final form.

Copyright © 1980 by Incentive Publications, Inc. All Rights Reserved.
No part of this publication may be reproduced, stored in a retrieval
system, or transmitted, in any form or by any means, electronic, me-
chanical, photocopying, recording, or otherwise, without prior written
permission from Incentive Publications, Inc., with the exception listed
below.

All pattern pages and scripts are intended for reproduction. Permission
is hereby granted to the purchaser to reproduce these pages in quantities
suitable for meeting yearly classroom needs.

Library of Congress Catalog Card Number: 80-80256
ISBN Number: 0-913916-66-8

Printed in Nashville, Tennessee
United States of America

The REAL Happily Ever After Book

This book contains 21 fairy tales written in dialogue form to be used in presenting puppet shows or plays. Each fairy tale is accompanied by a cut-and-paste activity. Some of the activities are masks, which the students may use in dramatizing the fairy tale. Others are finger puppets for a puppet show. Still others are follow-ups which the students may complete after listening to a tale.

For older students, duplicate the script for the fairy tale to be dramatized. Discuss the characters -- how they look, speak, act, and feel. (Talk about Little Red Riding Hood's feelings and facial expressions as she talked to the wolf when he was dressed up as her grandmother.) Discuss settings, and what different scenes may be needed. (In "Beauty and the Beast," two settings may be needed: the merchant's home and the beast's castle.) Discuss what props and costumes may be needed (such as the boots and game sack for the cat in "Puss in Boots").

For younger students, read the fairy tale aloud, give a puppet show, act out all the parts yourself, or use any one of a variety of story-telling techniques. Secure an illustrated copy of the fairy tale from your media center or local library to show to the students. If a copy is not available, adapt the script in this book. Here is a portion of the script from "Jack and the Beanstalk."

NARRATOR:	Once there lived a mother and her son, Jack. They were very poor.
MOTHER:	Jack, we have no money. Take the cow to town and sell her.
NARRATOR:	Jack had not gone far when he met a little man.
LITTLE MAN:	Young man, where are you going?
JACK:	I'm on my way to town to sell our cow.
LITTLE MAN:	I have here a bag of magic beans. I'll give them to you for your cow.

Reword the story in your own words, something like this:

Once there lived a mother and her son, Jack. They were very poor. One day, Jack's mother said to him, "Jack, we have no money. Take the cow to town and sell her."

So Jack set out for town. He had not gone far when he met a strange little man. The little man said, "Young man, where are you going?"

Jack answered, "I'm on the way to town to sell our cow."

The little man replied, "I have a bag of magic beans. I'll give them to you for your cow."

Read a story several times to the students. By the third reading, you may be able to let the students say any repetitive phrases. (For example, after hearing the story several times, the students will be able to say from memory, "Run, run, as fast as you can! You can't catch me, I'm the Gingerbread Man.") In this way, the whole class will learn the lines of each character.

You may wish to act as narrator and prompter when the play is presented, or choose a student for this part. The way in which the story is told should cue the actors as to what happens next. (For instance, in "Goldilocks and the Three Bears," notice as the narrator cues the actress to the next action:

NARRATOR: Then, she sat down in Baby Bear's chair.
GOLDILOCKS: This chair is just right!
NARRATOR: But all of a sudden, the chair began to rock and sway. Then it collapsed, and Goldilocks landed on the floor.

Because of the cue from the narrator, the actress knows that she should begin to rock the chair until it falls.)

Make certain the students know that they are not restricted to the exact words of the script. They may improvise actions and dialogue as long as they stick to the basic plot.

At the end of each narrative, you will find the assembly directions for the supplemental cut-and-paste activity. When you pass out copies of the activity, give these directions to the students verbally. Have scissors, crayons, and paste available.

Creative dramatics can be a fun and rewarding activity for students. Those who do poorly in academic subjects have an opportunity to experience success through acting. Students who are discipline problems in the classroom will love having a chance to "ham it up" in an accepted setting. The shy student who is too scared to speak for himself can speak out through a puppet or a character in a play. All students will benefit from the organizational and social interaction skills they must develop to put on a play.

TABLE OF CONTENTS

Page

SNOW WHITE

NARRATOR:	Once a king had a little daughter who was the joy of his life. Her skin was white as snow, her lips as red as blood, and her hair was as black as night. The king's first wife had died, and he remarried. His second wife was very beautiful, but she was jealous of all the other pretty women in the kingdom. The queen had a magic mirror, and every day, she looked into it and asked...
QUEEN:	Mirror, mirror, on the wall, who is the fairest one of all?
MIRROR:	You are, O Queen.
NARRATOR:	If the magic mirror said that she was the fairest in the kingdom, the queen was happy. But if the mirror said another woman was more beautiful, the queen became furious. She would call her huntsman and have the other woman killed. As the years passed, Snow White grew more and more beautiful. So, one day when the queen asked her mirror...
QUEEN:	Mirror, mirror, on the wall, who is the fairest one of all?
MIRROR:	Queen, you are full fair, 'tis true, but Snow White is fairer still than you.
QUEEN:	Curse that child! Huntsman, come here at once. You are to take Snow White into the woods and kill her. Bring me back her heart to prove that she is dead.
HUNTSMAN:	Snow White, come with me. We are going for a walk in the woods.
NARRATOR:	Snow White and the huntsman walked deep into the forest. As they went, the huntsman said to himself...
HUNTSMAN:	I cannot kill this beautiful child. I'll kill a squirrel instead, and take its heart to the queen.
NARRATOR:	The huntsman left Snow White alone in the woods. Lost, Snow White stumbled deeper into the forest. At last, she came to a small cottage. No one was home, so she went inside.
SNOW WHITE:	Why, look at this place. It's full of tiny furniture! But there's a layer of dust on everything, and the sink is full of dirty little cups and plates! Maybe the children who live here have no mother. I'll wash and clean things for a surprise. Then maybe they'll let me stay and keep house for them!
NARRATOR:	Soon Snow White had the house spic and span.
SNOW WHITE:	Let me see what's upstairs. Why, seven little beds in a row! Hmm, I'm a bit sleepy. I'll take a little nap.
NARRATOR:	Snow White lay down across the beds and was soon asleep. When it was getting dark, the little men who lived in the house came home.
DWARF #1:	Look, there's smoke coming out of the chimney! Someone is in our house!

DWARF #2:   Come on, maybe he's still here! Look! Someone has stolen all our dishes!

DWARF #3:   Our dishes haven't been stolen. See, someone has washed them all!

NARRATOR: Just then, Snow White awoke and saw the dwarves.

SNOW WHITE: Oh, you're not children! You're little men! The wicked queen sent me out into the woods to die. May I stay here with you?

DWARF #4:   You may stay if you will cook and clean for us.

NARRATOR: Back at the castle, the huntsman gave the squirrel heart to the queen.

QUEEN: Now, mirror, mirror, on the wall, who is the fairest one of all?

MIRROR: Queen, you are a beauty rare, but Snow White, living in the glen with seven little men, is a thousand times more fair!

QUEEN: Ooh! That huntsman! He tricked me! Well, I'll have to take care of Snow White myself. I'll dress in rags like an old woman. Then I'll make a poisoned apple and give it to Snow White, and she will eat it and die! Ha, ha, ha, ha!

NARRATOR: The queen put the apple in a basket and went to the house of the seven dwarves.

QUEEN: Please, can you give an old woman a drink of water?

SNOW WHITE: Why, of course. Here you are.

QUEEN: Thank you, my dear. Now, you must take this beautiful apple in return.

NARRATOR: Snow White took the poisoned apple. She bit into it and fell down, lifeless. When the dwarves came home, they found her. They put her in a glass box and set it on the mountain. There they kept watch day and night. One day, a handsome prince came upon Snow White as he rode through the forest. He lifted the glass lid, and tilted her head back to kiss her on the lips. This kiss broke the spell of the wicked queen, and she opened her eyes. The seven dwarves danced for joy. Then, the prince carried Snow White off to his castle on his white charger. Snow White and the prince were married, and they all lived happily ever after.

Assembly Directions for Pages 9 and 11

1. Color all figures and cut them out.
2. Curve the two sides of each puppet around to the back and paste.
3. Curve Snow White's skirt around to the back. Overlap to dotted line and paste.
4. Fold the prince cut-out on dotted lines, leaving horse head and top of body standing up.

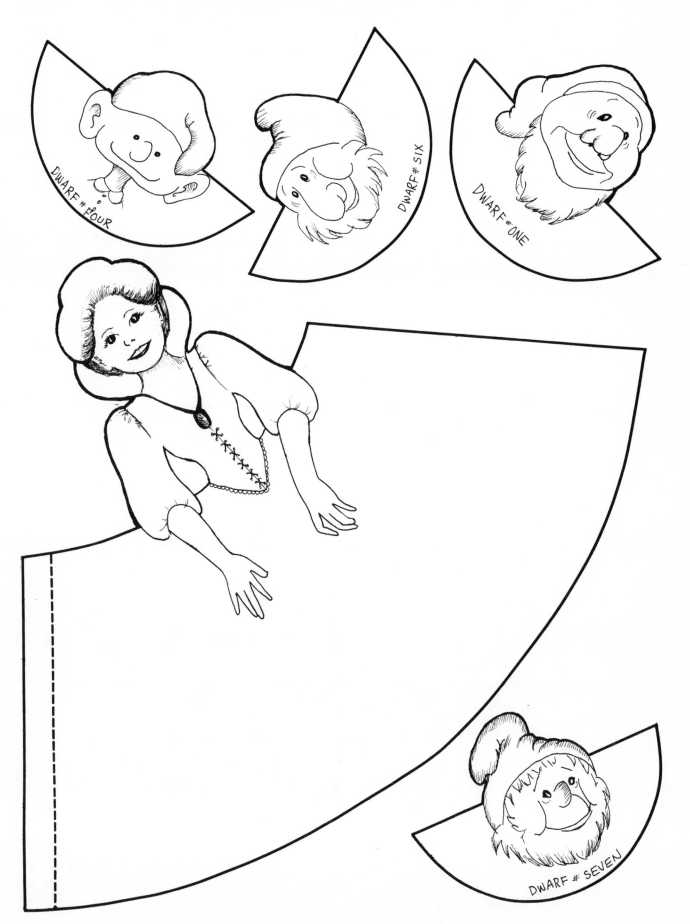

DWARF # FOUR

DWARF # SIX

DWARF # ONE

DWARF # SEVEN

THE LITTLE MERMAID

NARRATOR: Far below the sea lived the Sea King with his six beautiful daughters. They were all lovely, but the youngest was the prettiest of them all. Like the others, she had no feet, only a fish's tail, for she was a mermaid. All her sisters were happy and contented in their ocean home, but the little mermaid longed to hear stories about the world of human beings.

One evening, the little mermaid swam up to the surface of the sea. A terrible storm was raging. Angry waves tossed a ship back and forth. Suddenly, a huge wave washed a handsome prince overboard.

The little mermaid quickly swam to rescue the prince. She held his head above water and let the waves carry them to shore. She placed the prince on the sand and then swam back out to sea. She watched to see if someone would come to help the prince. Before long, a lovely black-haired girl came wandering toward the beach from a nearby religious building and found the prince. When the prince came to, he smiled at the young girl, as he thought she had saved him. He promised himself that he would marry her, for he knew nothing of the little mermaid.

The mermaid could think of nothing but the handsome prince. She longed to be with him. She wanted to marry him and live with him as a human being. Finally, she went to visit the Sea Witch.

SEA WITCH: I know why you have come, my pretty one. You want me to turn your fish tail into human limbs, so the prince will fall in love with you. I will brew a potion for you. It will make your tail part in two and shrink into legs. You will keep your gliding motion, but every step will feel like you are walking on sharp knives. Do you think you can bear it?

MERMAID: I can stand anything for my prince!

SEA WITCH: But you will have to pay me. You must give me your lovely voice.

MERMAID: If that is what you ask, then that shall be your payment.

SEA WITCH: All right, then. Put out your little tongue, and I will cut it out and take it as my fee. In return, I will drop my own blood into the potion to make it doubly sharp.

NARRATOR: With that, the witch finished the brew and gave the potion to the little mermaid. The mermaid swam to shore and drank the bubbling potion. The sharp pain it brought made her faint in agony. When she awoke, the handsome young prince was standing at her side.

PRINCE: Who are you? How did you come to be here?

NARRATOR: The little mermaid looked up at him with her beautiful dark eyes, but she could not speak. The prince took her hand and led her to the palace. He gave her lovely silken robes

13

to wear. That evening, the little mermaid danced for all the palace to see. Everyone was enchanted.

PRINCE: You must always remain with me. You will be given a velvet cushion so you can sleep outside my door. I will have a page's dress made up for you.

NARRATOR: The prince loved the little mermaid as one loves a dear, good child, but he had no thought of marrying her. He could only love the black-haired girl whom he thought had rescued him. But he knew she belonged to the religious order and could never marry anyone. Then one day, the prince's parents told him they were all going to visit a neighboring kingdom to meet the princess.

PRINCE: I must go see the beautiful princess. But I cannot love her. She is not like the beautiful maiden from the temple.

NARRATOR: The little mermaid accompanied the prince and his family. Their ship arrived, but the princess was not yet there. She was coming from the holy temple where she had received her education. At last she came.

PRINCE: It is you! The girl who saved me from the shipwreck! This is more than I could hope for. We shall be wed in the morning!

NARRATOR: The little mermaid felt that her heart was breaking. She now knew that she could never win the prince's love. So she threw her body into the sea, her true home.

Assembly Directions for Page 15

1. Color and cut out mermaid and skirt.
2. Cut slit and circle on skirt.
3. Put a paper fastener through the mermaid's belly button.
4. Slide skirt under head of paper fastener.
5. For a mermaid tail that moves, cut the tail off along the "V." Paste a small piece of paper onto the top of the tail from the back. Make a slit and circle like the one on the skirt. Slip the tail behind the paper fastener.

15

PUSS IN BOOTS

NARRATOR: Once upon a time there was a poor miller. When he died, he left his mill to his eldest son, his donkey to his second son, and his cat to his youngest son.

YOUNGEST SON: What good can a cat be? After I eat him and make a muff from his fur, I will have nothing left. I will surely die of hunger.

PUSS IN BOOTS: You haven't done so poorly, Master. Give me a pair of boots and a bag. You'll see that I'm not as useless as you think.

NARRATOR: Puss in Boots went into the woods. He put some lettuce and carrots in his bag. Opening it, he put the bag near a rabbit warren. Soon two rabbits were trapped in the bag. Puss in Boots took the bag to the king.

PUSS IN BOOTS: Here is a gift for you from my master, the Marquis de Carabas.

KING: Thank your master, and tell him that I am pleased with his gift.

NARRATOR: Puss in Boots continued to bring presents to the king. Each time, he told the king that they were from his master, the Marquis de Carabas. One day, the king decided to take his beautiful daughter for a ride along the river. Puss in Boots learned of this, and ran to his master.

PUSS IN BOOTS: Master, go quickly and wash in the river, and your fortune will be made.

NARRATOR: The miller's son did as he was told. When the king came riding by, Puss in Boots cried out...

PUSS IN BOOTS: Help! Help! Thieves have robbed my master and thrown him in the river! If he does not get help soon, the Marquis de Carabas will drown!

NARRATOR: The king remembered the fine gifts that the Marquis de Carabas had given him.

KING: Hurry, men! Pull my loyal Marquis out of the river! Officers of the Wardrobe! Run quickly! Bring some fine clothes for the Marquis to wear.

NARRATOR: Soon the miller's son was dressed in the king's own fine clothes.

KING: Come, ride with my daughter and me in our carriage.

NARRATOR: Meanwhile, Puss in Boots ran ahead. He came to some farmers.

PUSS IN BOOTS: The king will come by in his carriage soon. Tell him these fields belong to the Marquis de Carabas, or you will be chopped to pieces!

NARRATOR: Soon, the king came riding by.

KING: Who owns these fine lands?

FARMERS: They belong to the Marquis de Carabas.

KING: You own many fine fields, Marquis.

NARRATOR:	Puss in Boots ran on, and told all he met to tell the king the same thing about their fields.
KING:	My friend, the Marquis de Carabas, you are to be congratulated for these fine fields. You must be a very rich lord.
NARRATOR:	Next, Puss in Boots ran ahead to a big castle that was owned by an ogre.
PUSS IN BOOTS:	I have heard that you can change yourself into any kind of creature you wish. But I cannot believe it until I see it.
OGRE:	It IS true! And to show you, I will turn myself into a lion. (Changes into a lion.) RRoarr! (Changes back.) You see!
PUSS IN BOOTS:	I have also heard that you can change yourself into the smallest animal -- such as a rat or a mouse. Clearly, this is impossible.
OGRE:	Ridiculous! Of course, I can do that, too! Watch, and you will see.
NARRATOR:	With that, the ogre turned himself into a tiny mouse. Puss in Boots pounced on him and ate him up. By this time, the king's carriage was passing the castle. Puss in Boots came out on the drawbridge.
PUSS IN BOOTS:	Welcome to the castle of the Marquis de Carabas!
KING:	What! My lord Marquis also owns this castle? There can be no finer palace. My daughter must marry such a grand lord!
NARRATOR:	So the princess and the Marquis were married. The miller's son was now a real lord. He lived with his princess and Puss in Boots in the ogre's great palace happily ever after.

Assembly Directions for Page 19
1. Color all figures, and cut them out.
2. Cut slit in hat. Slip hat over cat's head, leaving one ear in front of hat.
3. Cut slits in boots.
4. Fold boots down along center fold.
5. Fold flaps under the boots up.
6. Slide cat's feet into slits of boots.

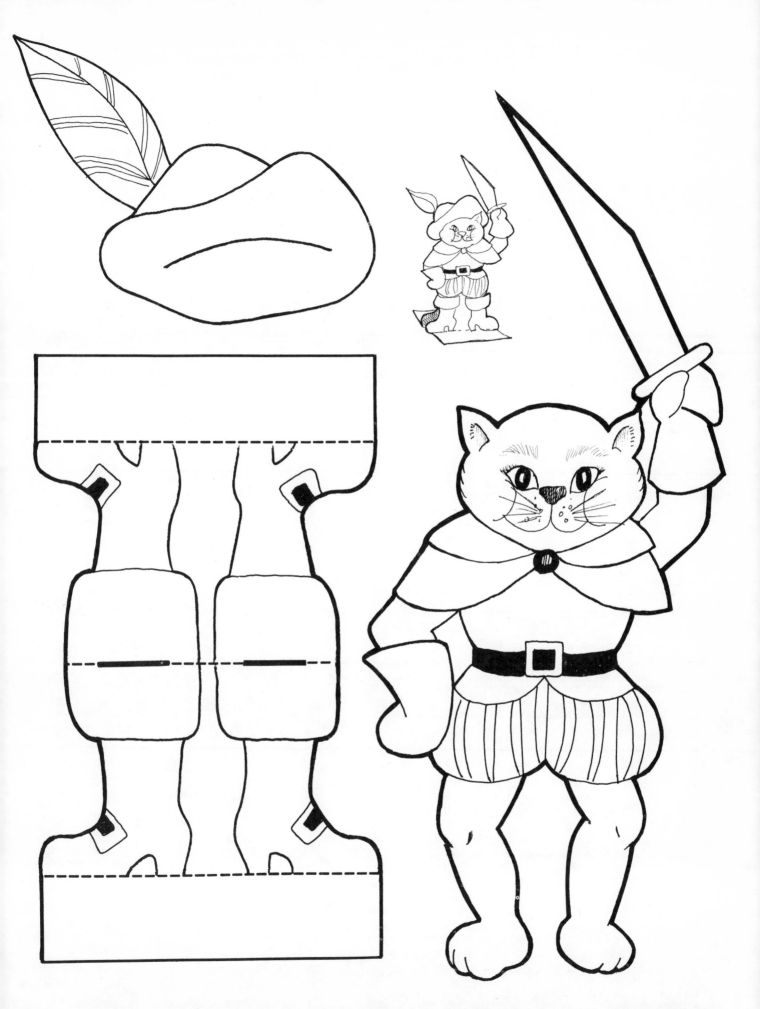

CHICKEN LICKEN

NARRATOR: One day, Chicken Licken was pecking for corn in the barnyard. All of a sudden, BOP! An acorn fell and hit her on the head.

CHICKEN LICKEN: Cluck! Cluck! Cluck, cluck, cluck! Oh, my goodness! The sky is falling! I must go and tell the king!

NARRATOR: So Chicken Licken started down the road to the king's palace. As she was walking, she met Cocky Locky.

COCKY LOCKY: Cock-a-doodle-do! Where are you going this fine morning?

CHICKEN LICKEN: I'm going to tell the king that the sky is falling!

COCKY LOCKY: Cock-a-doodle-do! I think I'll come along with you!

NARRATOR: So Chicken Licken and Cocky Locky went to tell the king that the sky was falling. While they were walking, they met Ducky Lucky.

DUCKY LUCKY: Quack! Quack! Where are you going this fine morning?

CHICKEN LICKEN
& COCKY LOCKY: We're going to tell the king that the sky is falling.

DUCKY LUCKY: Quack! I think I'll go along with you.

NARRATOR: So Chicken Licken and Cocky Locky and Ducky Lucky went to tell the king that the sky was falling. Soon, they met Goosey Loosey.

GOOSEY LOOSEY: Honk! Honk! Where are you going this fine morning?

CHICKEN LICKEN,
COCKY LOCKY, &
DUCKY LUCKY: We're going to tell the king that the sky is falling.

GOOSEY LOOSEY: Honk! I think I'll go along with you.

NARRATOR: So Chicken Licken, Cocky Locky, Ducky Lucky, and Goosey Loosey went to tell the king that the sky was falling. Soon, they met Turkey Lurkey.

TURKEY LURKEY: Gobble, gobble! Where are you going this fine morning?

CHICKEN LICKEN,
COCKY LOCKY,
DUCKY LUCKY, &
GOOSEY LOOSEY: We're going to tell the king that the sky is falling.

TURKEY LURKEY: Gobble! I think I'll go along with you.

NARRATOR: So Chicken Licken, Cocky Locky, Ducky Lucky, Goosey Loosey, and Turkey Lurkey went to tell the king that the sky was falling. While they were walking, they met Foxy Loxy.

FOXY LOXY: Where are you going this fine morning?

ALL: (Cluck! Cock-a-doodle-do! Quack! Honk, honk! Gobble, gobble!) We're going to tell the king that the sky is falling.

FOXY LOXY: But you're not going in the right direction! Do you want me to show you the way?

ALL: (Cluck! Cock-a-doodle-do! Quack! Honk, honk! Gobble, gobble!) Yes, please show us where to go.

NARRATOR: So Chicken Licken, Cocky Locky, Ducky Lucky, Goosey Loosey, and Turkey Lurkey followed Foxy Loxy through the forest. They walked along until they came to a dark hole in the side of the hill.

FOXY LOXY: This is a short cut to the king's palace. Follow me.

NARRATOR: So Chicken Licken, Cocky Locky, Ducky Lucky, Goosey Loosey, and Turkey Lureky followed Foxy Loxy into the hole. But the hole was actually Foxy Loxy's den, and Chicken Licken, Cocky Locky, Ducky Lucky, Goosey Loosey, and Turkey Lurkey made a delicious dinner for Foxy Loxy and his family. And the king never knew that the sky had fallen.

Assembly Directions for Page 23
1. Color all figures and cut them out.
2. Fold stands back on dotted lines.
3. Stand animals up on flat surface.

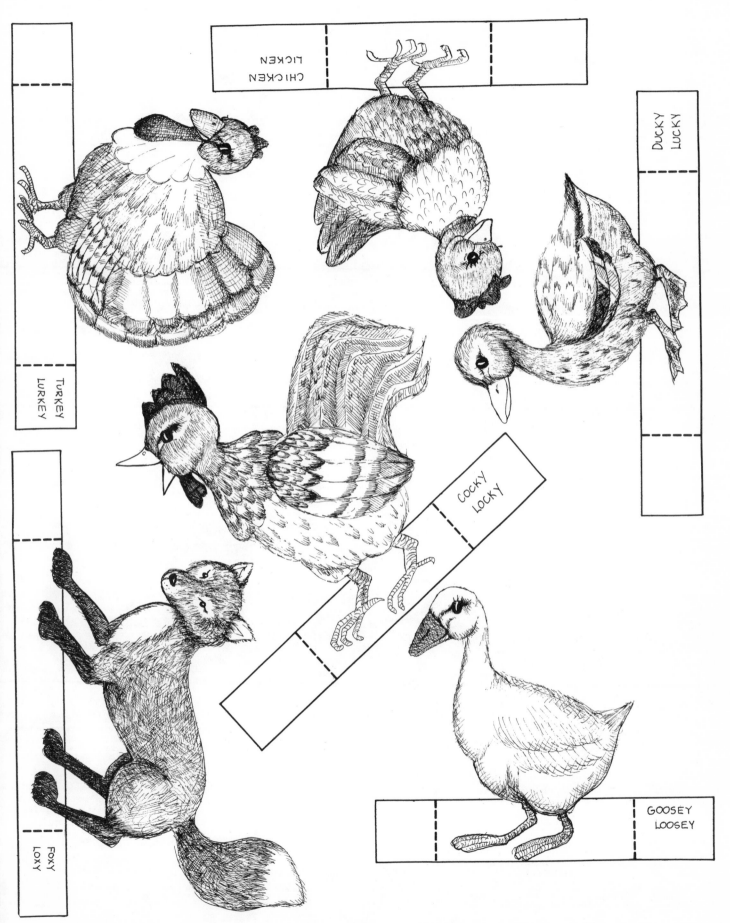

CHICKEN LICKEN

DUCKY LUCKY

TURKEY LURKEY

COCKY LOCKY

FOXY LOXY

GOOSEY LOOSEY

23

THE UGLY DUCKLING

NARRATOR:	It was summer in the country. Down by the lake, nestled among the leaves, a mother duck sat upon her nest.
MOTHER DUCK:	I'm so tired of sitting. Won't my eggs ever hatch?
NARRATOR:	At last the eggs began to crack. One after another, the baby ducklings poked their heads out.
DUCKLINGS:	Cheep! Cheep! How big the world is!
MOTHER DUCK:	I suppose you are all here now? No, that big egg hasn't cracked yet. I wonder how much longer it will last.
NARRATOR:	Then, the mother duck sat down to wait for the last egg to crack. A little while later, an old duck came to pay her a visit.
OLD DUCK:	How are you doing, Mother Duck?
MOTHER DUCK:	This last egg is taking such a long time. I'm tired of sitting on it. But you must look at my others -- they're such fine ducklings.
OLD DUCK:	Let me look at the egg that won't crack. Why, I'll bet that's a turkey's egg! I was cheated like that once. It means trouble and worry, for turkey chicks are afraid of the water. Yes, that's a turkey's egg, all right. Leave it alone, and teach the other children to swim.
MOTHER DUCK:	I've sat on the egg this long; I might as well sit on it a little longer.
OLD DUCK:	Suit yourself.
NARRATOR:	And away went the old duck. Mother Duck sat and sat. At last, the big egg cracked.
UGLY DUCKLING:	Cheep! Cheep!
NARRATOR:	Out tumbled the young one. How big and ugly he was!
MOTHER DUCK:	What a monstrous big duckling. None of the others looked like that! I wonder if he is a turkey chick. Well, we'll soon find out.
NARRATOR:	With that, the mother duck pushed the ugly duckling into the water.
MOTHER DUCK:	Quack! Quack! Well, what do you know? He swims beautifully. He must be my own duck after all! Now, ducklings, come with me so I can introduce you to the animals in the barn yard.
ANIMALS:	Oh, my! Look at that big duckling. How ugly he is! We don't want him around here!!
NARRATOR:	Then the ducks flew at him and bit him, and the chickens pecked at him.
MOTHER DUCK:	Leave him alone! He isn't doing any harm!!

(The following portion may be pantomimed as the narrator reads aloud.)

NARRATOR:	Even his brothers and sisters made fun of the ugly duckling. He did not know what to do, so he ran

NARRATOR (con't): through the bushes to the reeds by the lake. Even here, the ugly duckling could find no peace. The wild ducks and geese also made fun of him. Sadly, the ugly duckling passed the summer.

Now, the leaves were turning yellow and brown. One autumn day, a flock of beautiful white birds came to the lake. The ugly duckling thought he had never seen such lovely creatures. They were swans. The duckling felt strangely drawn to them, but he did not know why. He dove down under the surface so that they would not see his ugliness.

Winter came, and the air grew cold. The lake began to freeze. The ugly duckling had to keep swimming about to keep from freezing. At last, he became too tired to swim, and was frozen fast in the ice. In the early morning, an old woman came along and saw him. She hit the ice with her shoe and broke it, setting the duckling free. Then she carried him home and set him in front of the fire to warm. It was there in the old woman's house that the ugly duckling spent the winter.

Spring finally arrived, and the ugly duckling went again to the lake to swim. He raised his wings, and they flapped with much greater strength than before. Just in front of him, he saw three beautiful white swans. He lowered his head in shame at his ugliness. But what did he see reflected in the water? His own image was that of a swan! The new swan felt shy and happy. He did not regret all the misery he had been through, for it only made him appreciate his good fortune more now. He joined the other swans, and they all lived happily ever after.

Assembly Directions for Page 27
1. Color all figures and cut them out.
2. Fold on dotted lines.
3. Paste two swan heads together.
4. Paste two duckling heads together (both sets).
5. Paste wings onto swan as marked.

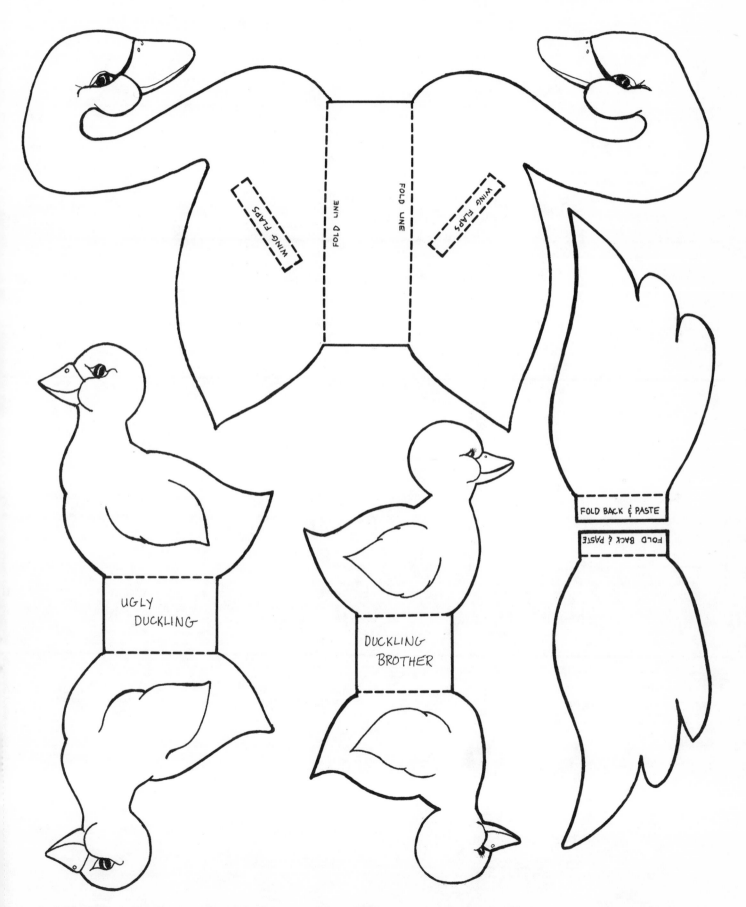

WING FLAPS

FOLD LINE

FOLD LINE

WING FLAPS

FOLD BACK & PASTE

FOLD BACK & PASTE

UGLY DUCKLING

DUCKLING BROTHER

THE ELVES AND THE SHOEMAKER

NARRATOR: There was once a kind old shoemaker. Through no fault of his own, he became very poor.

SHOEMAKER: I have only enough leather left to make one more pair of shoes. I will cut the leather tonight, and make the shoes in the morning.

NARRATOR: The shoemaker went to bed. The next morning, he went to his workbench.

SHOEMAKER: Well, what do you know! Come here, Wife. Someone has already made the leather into a pair of shoes!

WIFE: What a perfect pair of shoes! See the fine stitching? What fine quality.

NARRATOR: Soon, a customer came into the shoe shop.

CUSTOMER: What a finely made pair of shoes. Let me try them on. They fit perfectly! How much do you want for them? Here, I'll pay you double.

NARRATOR: After the customer left, the shoemaker said to his wife...

SHOEMAKER: Now I have enough money to buy leather for two more pairs of shoes!

WIFE: Good! Why don't you cut them out tonight, and then we'll go to bed.

NARRATOR: The next morning, the shoemaker again found that the leather had been made into shoes.

SHOEMAKER: Come here, Wife! Look at these dainty dancing slippers, and these elegant boots! Aren't they fine?

NARRATOR: Soon, a lady and a gentleman entered the shop.

LADY: What lovely dancing shoes! I must have them for the ball this weekend.

GENTLEMAN: These riding boots are an excellent fit. I'll take them.

SHOEMAKER: Now I have enough money to buy leather to make four pairs of shoes. I will begin cutting them out tonight.

NARRATOR: Early the next morning, the shoemaker found four pairs of finished shoes. And so it went. Each evening, the shoemaker cut out the leather. Each morning, the shoes were finished. Soon the shoemaker and his wife were making a good living.

WIFE: I have an idea, Husband. Let us stay up tonight to see who is making the shoes.

NARRATOR: That night, they hid in a corner of the shop. As the clock struck midnight, in came two little elves. They hopped up onto the workbench and set busily to work, singing all the while.

ELVES: La, la, la, la, la, la, la. La, la, la, la, la, la, la.

NARRATOR: In no time at all, the shoes were finished. Then the elves skipped out the window. The next morning, the shoemaker's wife said...

WIFE: The elves have made us wealthy. We should do something to show our thanks.

SHOEMAKER: Why don't you make them some tiny new clothes to wear. And I'll make them each a pair of shoes.

NARRATOR: A few nights later, the shoemaker and his wife laid out the presents on the workbench. Then they hid in the corner. At midnight, the elves came skipping and singing into the shop.

ELVES: La, la, la, la, la, la, la.

ELF #1: Look, Look! Tiny new clothes, just for us!

ELF #2: And a pair of shoes for each of us!

ELF #1: Hurry! Let's try them on!

NARRATOR: Laughing and singing, the elves slipped on the tiny new clothes and shoes. Then they danced about the shop and out the door. The elves came no more, but the good shoemaker and his wife lived happily ever after.

Assembly Directions for Page 31
1. Color all figures and cut them out.
2. Cut out circles for fingers.
3. Put fingers through holes, and move them as for hands and feet.

31

RAPUNZEL

NARRATOR: Once there lived a man and his wife. They had no child, but they wanted one very much. Next to them lived a witch who had a beautiful garden. One day, the wife saw some fresh green rampion in the witch's garden.

WIFE: Oh, Husband, I wish I had some of the witch's rampion. I want it so much that I cannot eat anything else. I am getting weak from hunger.

HUSBAND: I don't want you to be sick from lack of food. I will sneak into the witch's garden and get some for you.

NARRATOR: So the husband climbed the witch's fence, picked some rampion, and sneaked back to his wife.

WIFE: Oh, this is so good! I must have some more.

HUSBAND: I fear the witch's anger. But I will get some for you if you must have it.

NARRATOR: This time when the husband went to the witch's garden to steal the rampion, the witch was there.

WITCH: Stop, you thief! You won't get away with this. To make up for your stealing, you must give me your child when it is born.

HUSBAND: I'm so sorry, but my wife was sick with desire for your rampion. Let me go, and I'll promise you anything.

NARRATOR: The months passed, and the wife had a child.

WIFE: Isn't she a beautiful baby?

NARRATOR: Suddenly, the witch appeared.

WITCH: This child is mine now. Let me have it.

HUSBAND
& WIFE: No, no! Please, no!

WITCH: Your husband promised to give me your baby in place of the rampion which he stole. She is mine, and I name her Rapunzel.

NARRATOR: The witch took Rapunzel away. When she was twelve, the witch put her in a tower which had no steps or door, only a high, small window. When the witch wanted to come inside, she would call out...

WITCH: Rapunzel! Rapunzel! Let down your hair!

NARRATOR: Rapunzel had beautiful long golden hair. When she heard the witch call, she would lower her hair for the witch to climb up. Rapunzel was lonely in her tower, so she would sing to pass the time.

RAPUNZEL: Tra, la, la, la. Tra, la, la, la.

NARRATOR: One day, a king's son heard her sweet voice. As he stood there, hidden behind a tree, he saw the witch come and call out...

WITCH: Rapunzel! Rapunzel! Let down your hair!

NARRATOR: The prince watched as Rapunzel let down her long braid for the witch to climb. The next day, the prince re-turned and called out...

PRINCE: Rapunzel! Rapunzel! Let down your hair!

NARRATOR: Rapunzel thought that the witch was calling her, and let down her hair. When the prince climbed into the tower, Rapunzel was frightened.

RAPUNZEL: Oh! Who are you? I have never met a man before.

PRINCE: I heard your lovely singing, and I wanted to meet you. Won't you be my bride?

RAPUNZEL: You are much better looking than the witch. I will marry you. But how can I get out of the tower? I can't climb down on my own hair.

PRINCE: I will return with a rope. I must leave you now, but I will return.

NARRATOR: The prince left, and the next morning, the witch returned.

WITCH: Rapunzel! Rapunzel! Let down your hair!

NARRATOR: The witch climbed into the tower.

RAPUNZEL: Old Mother, how is it that you climb up here so slowly, but the Prince is with me in a minute?

WITCH: You wicked girl! You will pay for your trickery! I will cut off your hair!

NARRATOR: The witch tied Rapunzel's cut braid to the window. Soon, the prince came, and called out...

PRINCE: Rapunzel! Rapunzel! Let down your hair!

NARRATOR: The witch let the hair down. When the prince climbed up and saw the cruel witch instead of his dear Rapunzel, he jumped from the tower.

PRINCE: Aaah! My eyes, my eyes! I have landed in a sticker bush! I can't see! I am blinded!

NARRATOR: With his sight gone, the prince wandered blindly away. After what seemed like forever, he heard a familiar voice singing...

RAPUNZEL: Tra, la, la. Tra, la, la, la, la.

PRINCE: Oh, my Rapunzel! I have found you!

NARRATOR: Rapunzel's tears of happiness fell on the prince's blind eyes, and they became clear again.

PRINCE: I can see again! Come with me, my Rapunzel, and we will be married at last.

NARRATOR: So Rapunzel and the prince were married, and lived happily ever after.

Assembly Directions for Page 35

1. Color roof and tower, and cut them out.
2. Form roof into a cone shape and paste.
3. Form tower into a cylinder and paste.
4. Set roof on tower.

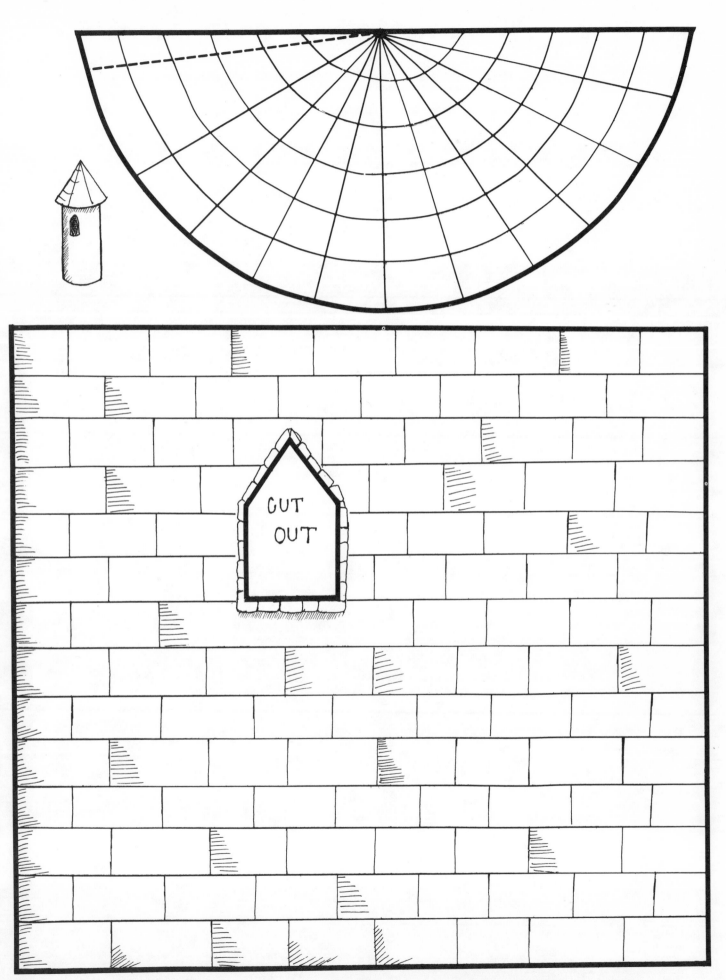

CUT OUT

THE GREAT BIG ENORMOUS TURNIP

NARRATOR: Once upon a time, an old man planted a turnip seed.

OLD MAN: Grow, little turnip, grow. Grow sweet. Grow strong.

NARRATOR: As the days passed, the seed grew into the biggest, most beautiful turnip the old man had ever seen. One day, the old man started to pull the turnip out of the ground. He pulled and pulled, but he could not pull it up. So he called for help.

OLD MAN: Old woman! Come help me pull up this turnip!

NARRATOR: The old woman pulled the old man. The old man pulled the turnip. They pulled and pulled, but they could not pull it up. So the old woman called for help.

OLD WOMAN: Granddaughter! Come help us pull up this turnip.

NARRATOR: The granddaughter pulled the old woman. The old woman pulled the old man. The old man pulled the turnip. They pulled and pulled, but they could not pull it up. So the granddaughter called for help.

GRANDDAUGHTER: Here, dog! Here, dog! Come help us pull up this turnip.

NARRATOR: The dog pulled the granddaughter. The granddaughter pulled the old woman. The old woman pulled the old man. The old man pulled the turnip. They pulled and pulled, but they could not pull it up. So the dog called for help.

DOG: Here, kitty! Here, kitty! Come help us pull up this turnip.

NARRATOR: The cat pulled the dog. The dog pulled the granddaughter. The granddaughter pulled the old woman. The old woman pulled the old man. They pulled and pulled, but they could not pull it up. So the cat called the mouse.

CAT: Here, mouse! Here, mouse! Come help us pull up this turnip.

NARRATOR: The mouse pulled the cat. The cat pulled the dog. The dog pulled the granddaughter. The granddaughter pulled the old woman. The old woman pulled the old man. The old man pulled the turnip. They pulled, and pulled, and pulled again. And up came the turnip!!

Assembly Directions for Page 39
1. Color all figures and cut them out.
2. Curve the two sides of each puppet around to the back and paste.
3. Put puppets on fingers and wiggle them.

HANSEL AND GRETEL

NARRATOR: Near the edge of a great forest lived a poor woodcutter with his wife and two children. The boy's name was Hansel, and the girl's name was Gretel. One night, the woodcutter said to his wife...

WOODCUTTER: What is to become of us? We are so poor that we don't even have enough money to buy food for our children.

WIFE: Here is what we must do. Tomorrow, we will take the children deep into the forest and leave them there. That will make two less mouths to feed.

WOODCUTTER: I cannot leave my children in the woods! Wild animals would soon eat them.

WIFE: If you don't leave them in the woods, all four of us will die of starvation.

NARRATOR: The mean step-mother would give her husband no peace until he agreed. But Hansel and Gretel had been lying awake in the next room, listening. Gretel was afraid, but Hansel told her...

HANSEL: Don't worry, Gretel. When our parents are asleep, I will go outside and fill my pockets with shiny white pebbles. Tomorrow, when they take us into the forest, I will leave a path of pebbles for us to follow.

NARRATOR: The next day, Hansel and Gretel went with their parents to the middle of the forest. Their father built a fire and left them there. When the moon came up, they followed the pebbles home. Their father was glad to see them, but the next night, their step-mother said...

WIFE: We have only half a loaf of bread left. We cannot feed the children. We will have to take them farther into the woods so that they won't be able to find their way back.

NARRATOR: Late that night, Hansel tried to get more pebbles, but the step-mother had locked the door. So the next day, Hansel had only bread crumbs to drop for their path. The woman led the children far into the woods. Their father built a fire. Then the step-mother said...

WIFE: Sit by the fire and rest. When we have finished cutting wood, we will come for you.

NARRATOR: The children waited by the fire, but the woodcutter never came for them. When they tried to follow the bread crumbs home, they discovered that the birds had eaten them. The children wandered farther and farther into the woods until they came upon a small house. As they got closer, they saw that the house was made of ginger-bread, with frosting on the roof and windows of clear rock candy.

HANSEL: Oh, boy! Look at that house! I'm going to try a piece of the roof! You have some of this window to eat, Gretel. It's delicious!

NARRATOR:	A wicked witch lived in the house. She came to the door dressed as an old woman.
WITCH:	Nibble, nibble, like a mouse. Who is nibbling at my house?
HANSEL:	My name is Hansel, and this is my sister, Gretel.
WITCH:	You must be very hungry. Come inside and have some dinner. You don't have to eat my house!
NARRATOR:	The witch gave the children some good food to eat, and then showed them two little white beds, one for each of them to sleep in. But later that night, when they were fast asleep, the witch took Hansel and put him in a cage. The next morning, the witch shook Gretel and said...
WITCH:	Wake up, lazy girl! Go cook some food, and give it to your brother. When he is fat enough, I will eat him.
NARRATOR:	Each morning, the witch checked to see if Hansel were fat enough to eat. But her eyesight was poor, so Hansel held out a chicken bone instead of his finger for the old witch to check. Day after day went by, but Hansel did not seem to be getting any fatter. Finally, the old witch decided to eat him the way he was.
WITCH:	Gretel, check the oven. See if it is hot enough to bake the bread.
GRETEL:	I don't know how to do it. Will you show me?
WITCH:	You stupid goose! Watch me.
NARRATOR:	The witch stooped down and put her head in the oven. Then Gretel gave her a hard shove into the oven and shut the door. Gretel let Hansel out of his cage. They filled their pockets with the witch's gold and jewels, and set out for home. After a while, they came to a great lake. They could not cross it alone, but a great white duck took pity on them, and gave them a ride on her back. At last, they found their way home. Their father was overjoyed to see them. As for the step-mother, she had died while the children were gone. So with the witch's treasure, the family was no longer poor, and they all lived happily ever after.

Assembly Directions for Page 43

1. Color all figures and cut them out.
2. Cut door open on solid lines.
3. Fold door open on dotted line.
4. Paste witch in place behind door.

Note: See page 39 for additional puppets (woodcutter, wife, and Gretel) for "Hansel and Gretel" story. Follow directions given on page 38.

Paste behind door

THE PRINCESS WHO NEVER LAUGHED

NARRATOR: There was once a king who had only one daughter. She was such a happy little girl, always laughing, that anyone who looked at her would smile right back. But one day, the princess fell ill and no longer laughed. The king called for all his doctors and wizards and knights, but no one could cure her. In despair, the king finally proclaimed that whoever made the princess laugh would marry her and inherit his kingdom when he died.

In this same kingdom, there lived a man who had three sons. The time came for the sons to leave home and seek their fortunes. The oldest son was given a fine lunch, and set out along the road. When he sat down to eat his lunch, a little old man suddenly appeared.

OLD MAN: Please, young man, will you share a bit of your lunch with a hungry old man?

SON #1: Go away, you old beggar. Don't bother me.

NARRATOR: So the little old man left, and the eldest son finished his lunch and went on his way. Soon, the second son, who was also given a fine lunch, came down the road. As soon as he sat down to eat, the little old man appeared.

OLD MAN: Please, young man, will you share a bit of your lunch with a hungry old man?

SON #2: Go away, you old beggar. Don't bother me.

NARRATOR: The youngest son, whose name was Simon, was not as bright as his brothers, and his parents looked on him with little favor. So he was sent on his way with only a chunk of stale bread. When he sat down by the road to rest and eat, the little old man again appeared.

OLD MAN: Please, young man, will you share a bit of your lunch with a hungry old man?

SIMON: I will be happy to share my food with you.

NARRATOR: Now, the little old man was really a wizard with magical powers.

OLD MAN: Because you have been so kind, I want you to have this magic goose with feathers of gold.

NARRATOR: Simon thanked the old man and went on his way, carrying the goose. That evening, he stopped at an inn to spend the night. Now, the innkeeper had three daughters who took a fancy to the goose. When Simon fell asleep, the oldest daughter started to pluck a golden feather. Imagine her surprise when her hand stuck fast to the goose, and she could not get it loose!

SISTER #1: Help, sisters, help! My hand is stuck fast to this goose!

NARRATOR: The second sister tried to help, but she, too, became stuck when she touched her sister.

SISTER #1 &
SISTER #2: Help, sister! We cannot get away from this goose!

45

NARRATOR: As the third sister tried to pull her sisters away from the goose, she, too, became stuck fast. In the morning, Simon set off with the goose, ignoring the three girls who were stuck to each other and the goose. So wherever Simon went, they were forced to follow. They were crossing a field when they met a preacher.

PREACHER: Girls shouldn't run after young men!

NARRATOR: And he took the youngest by the hand to lead her away. But the instant he touched her, he stuck fast and had to follow. Before long, an altar boy came running up to them.

ALTAR BOY: (to preacher) Where are you going, sir? Did you forget that there's a baptism today?

NARRATOR: But the second his hands touched the preacher's robe, he also became stuck. As the strange procession went along, they met two farmers.

PREACHER &
ALTAR BOY: Help! Help! We are stuck fast and cannot get free!

NARRATOR: But as soon as the farmers touched the others, they, too, became stuck. So there were seven people caught behind Simon and his goose.

As Simon traveled on, he came to the king's palace, and passed by the window of the princess who never laughed. As soon as she saw the golden goose with the seven people stuck behind it, stumbling along and tripping on each other's heels, she clapped her hands together and began to laugh and laugh. So the king, in accordance with his promise, announced that Simon had won the princess, and they were married and lived happily ever after. But nobody knows what became of the goose and those who were stuck to it!

Assembly Directions for Page 47
1. Color and cut out mask and mouth strip.
2. Cut slits in face as indicated.
3. Put strip through top slit from the back.
4. Slide strip up and down to change the mouth.

JACK AND THE BEANSTALK

NARRATOR: Once there lived a mother and her son, Jack. They were very poor.

MOTHER: Jack, we have no money. Take the cow to town and sell her.

NARRATOR: Jack had not gone far when he met a little man.

LITTLE MAN: Young man, where are you going?

JACK: I'm on the way to town to sell our cow.

LITTLE MAN: I have here a bag of magic beans. I'll give them to you for your cow.

NARRATOR: Jack took the beans, and ran home to show his mother.

MOTHER: Jack, you stupid boy! You traded our cow for a bunch of worthless beans!

NARRATOR: With that, she threw the beans out of the window. The next morning, Jack looked out of the window and saw a giant beanstalk growing up into the clouds. He rushed outside and began to climb it. After a long time, he reached the top of the beanstalk and saw a huge castle nearby. He was hungry, so he knocked on the door. (Knock, Knock, Knock.) The giant's wife answered the door.

JACK: Please, may I have something to eat?

WIFE: Yes, little boy, come in. But do not let my husband find you here.

NARRATOR: Jack was eating some food when he heard the giant coming.

GIANT: Fee, fi, foe, fum. I smell the blood of an Englishman! Be he alive, or be he dead, I'll grind his bones to make my bread!

NARRATOR: Quickly, Jack found a hiding place.

GIANT: Bring me my dinner.

NARRATOR: The giant ate his meal. Then, he called to his wife...

GIANT: Bring me my magic hen, and be quick about it!

NARRATOR: The giant's wife brought the hen and set it on the table.

GIANT: Lay, hen, lay!

NARRATOR: As Jack watched, an egg of gold appeared on the table. When Jack saw the wonderful hen, he knew that it had been his father's hen. Jack's mother had told him that a giant stole the hen from their family years ago. The giant played with the egg of gold, and then he went to sleep. Jack came out of his hiding place and took the hen. Then he ran back to the beanstalk and climbed down. The next day, Jack went up the beanstalk again. He knocked on the door. (Knock, Knock, Knock.) The giant's wife again answered the door.

JACK: Please, may I have something to eat?

WIFE: You again? I let you in last night, and you repaid me by stealing my husband's magic hen! Go away!

NARRATOR: So Jack pretended to go away. Then he came back and hid in the castle.

GIANT: Fee, fi, foe, fum. I smell the blood of an Englishman. Be he alive, or be he dead, I'll grind his bones to make my bread!

WIFE: You only smell your dinner cooking. Eat your fill.

NARRATOR: The giant ate his meal. Then he called to his wife...

GIANT: Bring me my bags of gold and silver!

NARRATOR: Jack watched the giant count his treasure, and waited until he had fallen fast asleep. Then Jack took the money bags and climbed back down the beanstalk. The next day, Jack climbed up to the castle and hid again. When the giant came home, he said...

GIANT: Fee, fi, foe, fum. I smell the blood of an Englishman. Be he alive, or be he dead, I'll grind his bones to make my bread!

WIFE: Your dinner is ready. That's what you smell.

NARRATOR: The giant ate his meal and then called to his wife...

GIANT: Bring me my magic harp.

NARRATOR: The giant's wife set the magic harp on the table.

GIANT: Play, magic harp, play.

NARRATOR: The harp began to play beautiful music, and soon, the giant fell asleep. Jack took the harp and started down the beanstalk. But the harp began to sing out to the giant. He woke up and started down the beanstalk after Jack. As soon as Jack reached the ground, he grabbed an ax and chopped down the beanstalk. The giant fell, made a great hole in the ground, and disappeared into the earth. Jack and his mother now had the hen, the gold and silver, and the magic harp, so together they lived happily ever after.

1. Tell the story to the students while you overlap sheets of newspaper as shown. Place each sheet about 3/4 of the way over the preceding sheet.

2. Roll newspaper to form a tight tube 3" to 4" in diameter.

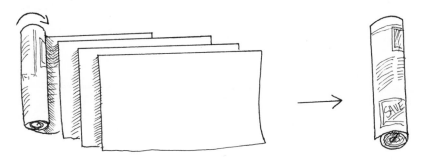

3. Make 3 or 4 strips, and rip them downward as you talk.

4. Reach into the center of the leaves, and grab the innermost layer. Holding the stalk in one hand, pull up on the leaves. Now you have a beanstalk.

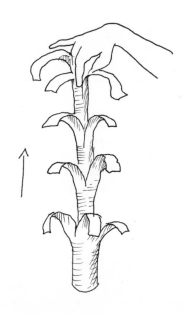

BEAUTY AND THE BEAST

NARRATOR: Once upon a time, there was a merchant who lived with his three daughters. His two older daughters, by his first marriage, were beautiful, but mean and conceited. But his youngest daughter was so kind and generous and modest, as well as beautiful, that everyone called her Beauty.

All of the merchant's ships had been captured by pirates, so the family was forced into poverty. Then one day, the merchant received a message.

MESSENGER: One of your ships escaped the pirates and will soon land!

MERCHANT: I must go to the harbor at once! My daughters, what gifts would you like me to bring you?

DAUGHTER #1: Bring me a velvet dress trimmed in gold.

DAUGHTER #2: I want a diamond necklace. And make sure the diamonds are big!

BEAUTY: All I need to make me happy, Father, is your safe return, and one red rose.

NARRATOR: When the poor merchant reached the harbor, he discovered that his richly laden ship had been seized to pay his debts, and he was just as poor as ever. Sadly, he started home. On his way, the merchant became lost in a terrible storm. He wandered blindly until he came to a great castle. The doors were open, so the merchant went inside. The table was set with a delicious meal, and the merchant ate his fill. Then he retired to a comfortable bedroom. The next day, when the merchant left, he walked out through a beautiful garden. Suddenly, he remembered Beauty's request for a rose.

MERCHANT: I could not bring back velvet dresses or diamond necklaces. But at least I can take a red rose for my Beauty. I'll pick this beautiful one for her.

NARRATOR: But when he did, an ugly beast dressed in the clothes of a prince suddenly appeared.

BEAST: You ungrateful man! I give you food and rest, and you repay my hospitality by picking my prize rose! You will die for this!

MERCHANT: Please forgive me! I only picked the rose to give to my daughter.

BEAST: Well, I will let you go only if one of your daughters comes willingly to take your place and live at my castle. Now, go!

NARRATOR: When the merchant returned home, he told his daughters of his misfortune.

BEAUTY: I will go, Father. It is my fault you took the rose.

NARRATOR: Beauty kissed her father farewell and began her journey. When Beauty arrived at the castle of the beast, she was treated well. The beast was kind, and soon Beauty lost her fear of him.

BEAST: Am I so terribly ugly?

BEAUTY: Yes, you are. But you are so kind and gentle that I don't mind your looks.

BEAST: Will you marry me and promise never to leave me?

BEAUTY: I cannot marry you, but if you will let me go visit my father, I will come back to you.

BEAST: You may go for three weeks, but if you do not return, I will die. Take this magic ring, and place it on your bed-side table when you are ready to go or return.

NARRATOR: That night, Beauty placed the ring on her table. In the morning, she awoke in her father's house.

MERCHANT: Beauty! I thought I'd never see you again! Are you all right? Has the beast harmed you? Are you home to stay?

BEAUTY: The beast would never hurt me. He is very kind and gen-tle. But I have only come home for a visit. I promised the beast that I would return.

NARRATOR: Beauty enjoyed her visit so much that she lost track of time. Then one night, she dreamed that the beast was lying dead in the palace garden.

BEAUTY: Oh, no! I must go to my beast before it is too late!

NARRATOR: Quickly, Beauty placed the magic ring on her bedside table. In no time, she was back at the palace garden. There was the beast, lying in the garden.

BEAUTY: Oh, my poor beast! Please don't die! I love you.

BEAST: Will you marry me, Beauty?

BEAUTY: Oh, yes!

NARRATOR: Just then, a dazzling light flashed. Instead of an ugly monster, a handsome young prince was lying in the garden.

BEAUTY: Who are you? And where is my good, kind beast?

PRINCE: I am your beast. A cruel spell was cast upon me, and I could not return to my own body until a beautiful girl promised to marry me in spite of my ugliness.

NARRATOR: The prince and Beauty were married in the rose garden, and Beauty's father came to live in the palace. The two greedy sisters were left to work the fields, so that the sun made their noses peel and the tools roughened their hands. But Beauty and her prince and her father all lived happily ever after.

Assembly Directions for Page 55
1. Color and cut out mask.
2. Cut out eyes, or prick several pin holes in eyes so user can see out.
3. Cut out mouth on solid line.
4. Cut out nose on solid line. Fold up on dotted line.
5. Punch holes for yarn. Tie around head.

THE LITTLE RED HEN

NARRATOR:	Once upon a time, a little red hen and her chicks lived in a cozy little house. They had three lazy neighbors — a pig, a duck, and a cat. All day long, the pig wallowed in the mud, the duck swam in her pond, and the cat slept in the sun. One day, as the little red hen was pecking about in the yard, she found a grain of wheat.
LITTLE RED HEN:	Who will plant this grain of wheat?
PIG:	Not I.
DUCK:	Not I.
CAT:	Not I.
LITTLE RED HEN:	Then I will.
NARRATOR:	And she did. The wheat grew and grew until it was tall and golden and ready to be harvested.
LITTLE RED HEN:	Who will harvest the wheat?
PIG:	Not I.
DUCK:	Not I.
CAT:	Not I.
LITTLE RED HEN:	Then I will.
NARRATOR:	And she did. The little red hen chopped down the wheat. Soon it was ready to be ground into flour.
LITTLE RED HEN:	Who will take this wheat to the mill for grinding?
PIG:	Not I.
DUCK:	Not I.
CAT:	Not I.
LITTLE RED HEN:	Then I will.
NARRATOR:	And she did. The little red hen carried the wheat to the mill and returned with a sack of fine white flour.
LITTLE RED HEN:	Who will make this flour into bread?
PIG:	Not I.
DUCK:	Not I.
CAT:	Not I.
LITTLE RED HEN:	Then I will.
NARRATOR:	And she did. The little red hen mixed and kneaded the dough and put it in the oven. Soon, the fine aroma of freshly baked bread filled the air. After a time, the little red hen took the bread from the oven.
LITTLE RED HEN:	Who will eat the bread?
PIG:	I will!
DUCK:	I will!
CAT:	I will!
LITTLE RED HEN:	Oh, no you won't! I found the grain of wheat. I planted it. I harvested the ripe grain. I took it to the mill. I baked the bread. My chicks and I will eat it all by ourselves!
NARRATOR:	And they did!

Assembly Directions for Page 59
1. Color and cut out masks.
2. Cut out eyes, or prick holes with
   a pin so user can see through.
3. Cut out duck bill on page 67. Paste
   to duck mask as marked.
4. Punch holes for yarn. Tie around
   head.

Note: See page 63 for additional masks for "The Little Red Hen" story.
       Follow directions given on page 62.

PASTE BILL HERE

PASTE BILL HERE

THE THREE LITTLE PIGS

NARRATOR: Once there were three little pigs. One day, they decided to leave home and build houses of their own. The first little pig built a house of straw. The second little pig build a house of sticks. The third little pig build a house of bricks.

One day, the big bad wolf came upon the straw house that belonged to the first little pig.

BIG BAD WOLF: Hmm. A little pig would make a good lunch for me. (Knock, knock, knock.) Little pig, little pig, let me come in!

LITTLE PIG #1: Not by the hair of my chinny-chin-chin!

BIG BAD WOLF: Then I'll huff and I'll puff and I'll blow your house in!

NARRATOR: So he huffed, and he puffed, and he blew the house in. But the first little pig got out the back way and ran to the house of the second little pig.

The next day, the big bad wolf came upon the house of sticks that belonged to the second little pig.

BIG BAD WOLF: (Knock, knock, knock.) Little pig, little pig, let me come in!

LITTLE PIG #2: Not by the hair of my chinny-chin-chin!

BIG BAD WOLF: Then I'll huff and I'll puff and I'll blow your house in!

NARRATOR: So he huffed, and he puffed, and he blew the house in. But the little pigs got out the back way and ran to the house of the third little pig.

The next day, the big bad wolf came upon the brick house that belonged to the third little pig.

BIG BAD WOLF: (Knock, knock, knock.) Little pig, little pig, let me come in!

LITTLE PIG #3: Not by the hair of my chinny-chin-chin!

BIG BAD WOLF: Then I'll huff and I'll puff and I'll blow your house in!

NARRATOR: So he huffed, and he puffed, and he huffed, and he puffed. But he could not blow the brick house down.

BIG BAD WOLF: Little pig, I'm going to climb on your roof and come down the chimney. Then I'm going to eat you up!

LITTLE PIG #3: Go ahead and try it!

NARRATOR: So the wolf climbed onto the roof. But the third little pig lit a fire in the fireplace and put a pot of water on to boil. The wolf slid down the chimney and landed SPLASH! in the pot. And that was the end of the big bad wolf.

THREE PIGS: (Sing.) Who's afraid of the big bad wolf, the big bad wolf, the big bad wolf? Who's afraid of the big bad wolf? Not us!!

NARRATOR: And they all lived happily ever after.

Assembly Directions for Page 63
1. Color and cut out all parts.
2. Cut out eyes, or prick with a
    pin so the user can see through
    the mask.
3. Fold beak and attach to hen
    mask as marked.
4. Punch holes for yarn. Tie
    around head.

Note: See page 67 for additional mask for "The Three Little Pigs"
       story. Follow directions given on page 66.

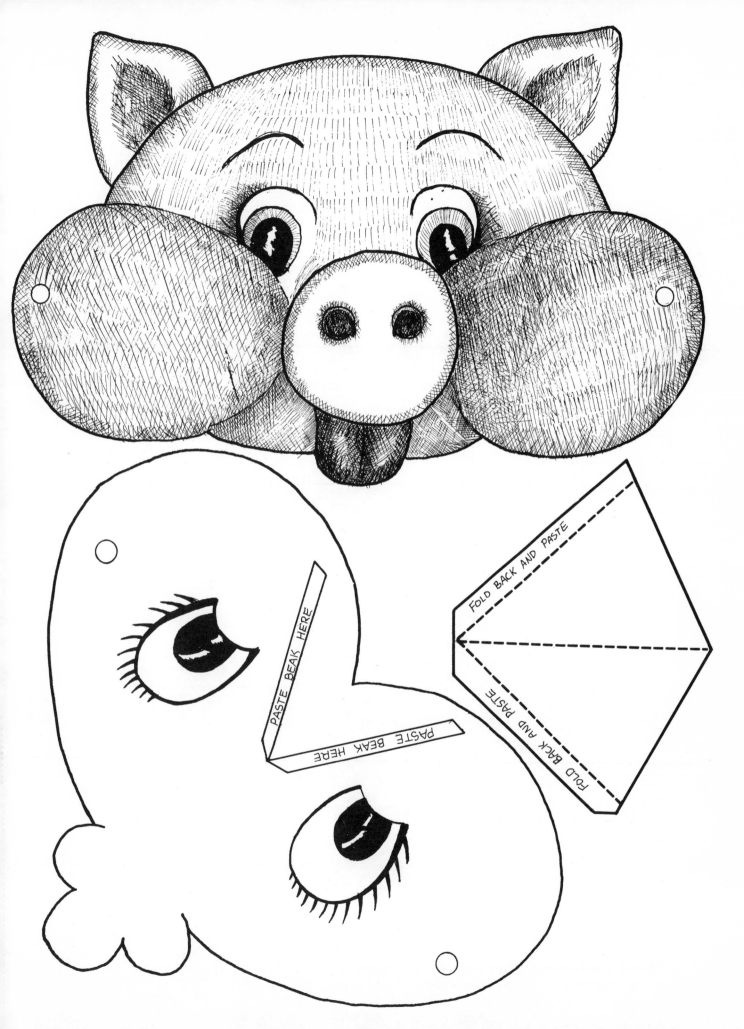

PASTE BEAK HERE

PASTE BEAK HERE

FOLD BACK AND PASTE

FOLD BACK AND PASTE

LITTLE RED RIDING HOOD

NARRATOR:	Once upon a time, a little girl lived with her mother in a tiny house at the edge of the forest. The little girl's grandmother, who lived deep in the woods, had made her a beautiful red cape and hood. The little girl wore it everywhere she went, so everyone called her "Little Red Riding Hood." One day, Little Red Riding Hood's mother said to her...
MOTHER:	Your grandmother is sick. Take her this basket of cookies and warm soup.
NARRATOR:	So Little Red Riding Hood set off through the forest. She hadn't gone very far when she met a wolf.
WOLF:	Where are you going, little girl?
RED RIDING HOOD:	I'm going to take this basket to my grandmother who is sick.
WOLF:	And where does your grandmother live?
RED RIDING HOOD:	In a little house deep in the woods.
WOLF:	Well, I'll go and visit her, too. I'll go this way, and you go that way. Then we'll see who gets there first.
NARRATOR:	The wolf took the shorter path and ran quickly to the grandmother's house. When he got there, he disguised his voice to sound like Little Red Riding Hood, and said...
WOLF:	Grandmother, it's Little Red Riding Hood. I've brought you a basket of soup and cookies.
GRANDMOTHER:	Well, lift up the latch and come in.
NARRATOR:	The wolf hurried in the door. He grabbed the grandmother, tied her up, and put her in the closet. Then he dressed himself in the grandmother's nightgown and cap. He lay down in the grandmother's bed, thinking how good Little Red Riding Hood would taste. Soon, Little Red Riding Hood knocked on the door.
WOLF:	Come in, Little Red Riding Hood.
NARRATOR:	The wolf spoke in an old lady voice. When Little Red Riding Hood saw her grandmother, she thought she looked very strange.
RED RIDING HOOD:	Oh, Grandmother, what big ears you have!
WOLF:	The better to hear you with, my dear.
RED RIDING HOOD:	Oh, but Grandmother, what big eyes you have!
WOLF:	The better to see you with, my dear.
RED RIDING HOOD:	Oh, but Grandmother, what big teeth you have!
WOLF:	The better to eat you with!
NARRATOR:	With that, the wolf jumbed out of the bed and gobbled up Little Red Riding Hood in one bite! His full belly made him sleepy, so he went back to bed.

SCHOOL OF EDUCATION
CURRICULUM LABORATORY
UM-DEARBORN

NARRATOR (con't.): Soon he began to snore loudly.

A woodcutter was passing by the house. When he heard the loud snoring, he went into the house to see if the old woman was all right. The woodcutter heard something bumping and pounding on the closet door. When he opened the door and saw the grandmother, he quickly set her free.

GRANDMOTHER: Oh woodcutter, thank you for saving me! But the wicked wolf has eaten Little Red Riding Hood! Can you do anything to save her?

WOODCUTTER: I can try!

NARRATOR: The woodcutter ran to the bed and killed the wolf. Then, he cut a long slit in the wolf's body, and out jumped Little Red Riding Hood! Little Red Riding Hood and her grandmother thanked the brave woodcutter. Then the woodcutter took the wolf's skin and went home. Little Red Riding Hood and her grandmother had the cookies and soup that she had brought to her grandmother, and they all lived happily ever after.

Assembly Directions for Page 67
1. Color all mask pieces and cut them them out.
2. Cut out eyes or prick holes with a pin so user can see through.
3. Fold nose down the center.
4. Fold back sides of nose and paste to mask as indicated.
5. Punch holes for yarn. Tie around head.

Notes: 1) Place a red towel or red crepe paper or red cloth around head and shoulders of actress and pin under chin to make red cloak and hood.

2) For a puppet show of "Little Red Riding Hood," use fox from page 23. Use granddaughter and old woman from page 39. Trace old woman and change face for the mother.

PASTE SNOUT HERE

PASTE SNOUT HERE

FOLD BACK AND PASTE

FOLD BACK AND PASTE

FOLD BACK AND PASTE

FOLD BACK AND PASTE

GOLDILOCKS AND THE THREE BEARS

NARRATOR: Once upon a time, there were three bears. There was a
              great big bear with a deep voice.
PAPA BEAR: Hello, I'm Papa Bear.
NARRATOR: There was a middle-sized bear.
MAMA BEAR: How do you do? I'm Mama Bear.
NARRATOR: And there was a little bear with a wee, tiny voice.
BABY BEAR: Hi, I'm Baby Bear.
NARRATOR: One morning, Mama Bear made some porridge. She
              called Baby Bear and Papa Bear to breakfast. Papa
              Bear tasted his porridge and said...
PAPA BEAR: This porridge is too hot!
MAMA BEAR: My porridge is too hot, too.
BABY BEAR: My porridge is too hot, too.
PAPA BEAR: Why don't we go for a walk while our porridge is cooling?
NARRATOR: So the bears put on their sweaters and went for a walk.
              On the other side of the woods lived a little girl named
              Goldilocks. One morning, she said to her mother...
GOLDILOCKS: Mother, may I go for a walk in the woods?
MOTHER: Yes, but don't go into any strange houses.
NARRATOR: So Goldilocks went skipping through the forest. Now and
              then, she stopped to pick flowers and whistle at the birds.
              After a while, Goldilocks came to a small house in
              the woods. She knocked on the door, but no one answered.
              She peeked in the window, but she didn't see anyone. She
              knocked on the door once more, but there was no answer.
              She tried the door. It wasn't locked, so she walked inside.
              She went over to the table and sat down in Papa Bear's
              place. She picked up his spoon and tasted his porridge.
GOLDILOCKS: This porridge is too hot.
NARRATOR: She left the spoon in the bowl instead of on the table where
              Papa Bear had left it. Next, she tried Mama Bear's
              porridge.
GOLDILOCKS: This porridge is too lumpy!
NARRATOR: Then she tried Baby Bear's porridge.
GOLDILOCKS: This porridge is just right.
NARRATOR: And she ate it all up. Then she went into the living room
              where she saw three chairs. She sat down in Papa Bear's
              chair.
GOLDILOCKS: This chair is too hard.
NARRATOR: Then she tried Mama Bear's chair.
GOLDILOCKS: This chair is too soft.
NARRATOR: Then she sat down in Baby Bear's chair.
GOLDILOCKS: This chair is just right!
NARRATOR: But all of a sudden, the chair began to rock and sway.
              Then it collapsed, and Goldilocks landed on the floor!
              So Goldilocks went upstairs to the bedroom. First, she
              tried Papa Bear's bed.

GOLDILOCKS: This bed is too hard.
NARRATOR: Then she tried Mama Bear's bed.
GOLDILOCKS: This bed is too soft.
NARRATOR: Then she tried Baby Bear's bed.
GOLDILOCKS: This bed is just right!
NARRATOR: And she fell fast asleep. Soon, the bears returned from their walk in the woods. They walked over to the table and sat down. Then Papa Bear saw that his spoon was not where he had left it!
PAPA BEAR: Someone's been eating my porridge.
MAMA BEAR: Someone's been eating my porridge, too!
BABY BEAR: Someone's been eating my porridge, and it's all gone!
NARRATOR: And Baby Bear began to cry. But Mama Bear said...
MAMA BEAR: That's okay, Baby Bear. I'll cook you some more.
PAPA BEAR: While we're waiting, let's go sit in the living room.
NARRATOR: So the bears went into the living room. Papa Bear looked at his chair and said...
PAPA BEAR: Someone's been sitting in my chair!
MAMA BEAR: Someone's been sitting in my chair, too!
BABY BEAR: Someone's been sitting in my chair, and they broke it all to pieces!
NARRATOR: And Baby Bear began to cry. But Papa Bear said...
PAPA BEAR: That's all right, Baby Bear. I can fix it.
NARRATOR: Then the three bears went upstairs. Papa Bear looked at his bed and said...
PAPA BEAR: Someone's been sleeping in my bed.
MAMA BEAR: Someone's been sleeping in my bed, too.
BABY BEAR: Someone's been sleeping in my bed, and there she is!
NARRATOR: Just then, Goldilocks woke up and saw the bears. She jumped out of bed, dashed down the stairs, and ran all the way home. When she got there, her mother asked...
MOTHER: Were you a good girl today?
GOLDILOCKS: Oh, Mother, I went into a strange house, but I learned my lesson, and I'll never do it again!
NARRATOR: So Goldilocks and her mother -- and the three bears--- all lived happily ever after!

Assembly Directions for Page 71
1. Color and cut out all parts.
2. Paste ears and snout on headband as shown.
3. Punch holes for yarn. Tie around head.
4. For Goldilocks, color the band yellow. Cut strips of yellow paper for hair. Paste them on headband and curl.

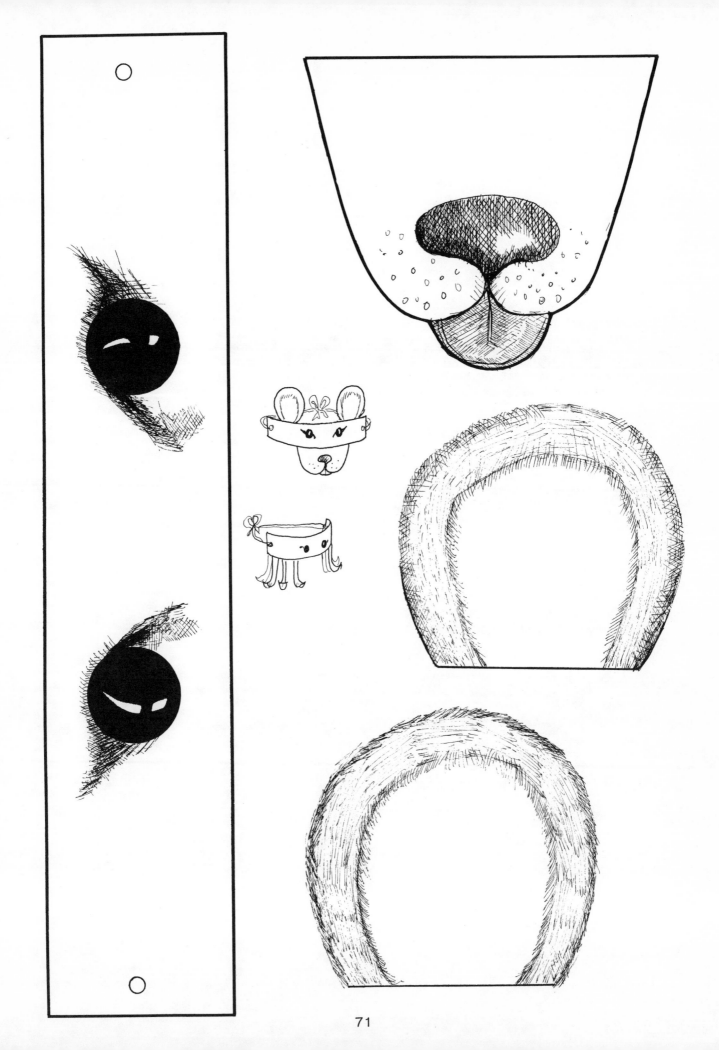

ROSE WHITE AND ROSE RED

NARRATOR: Once upon a time, a poor widow lived with her two daughters in a small cottage near the edge of the woods. Her daughters were as lovely as the roses that grew on the two rose bushes on either side of their front door. One was fair with fine white skin and pale hair. She was called Rose White. The other had red lips, raven black hair, and a lovely bloom in her cheeks. She was called Rose Red.
One cold winter night, a knock was heard at the door.

MOTHER: See who's knocking, Rose Red. Maybe it's a traveler who is lost in the darkness.

NARRATOR: Rose Red opened the door a crack. She peeked out and saw a big furry bear. Immediately she began to push the door shut, but the bear spoke.

BEAR: Do not fear, for I mean you no harm. I am freezing to death, and I would like to warm myself by your fire.

ROSE RED: Oh, you poor thing! Come in and sit by the fire.

BEAR: Thank you for your hospitality.

NARRATOR: The bear was so friendly and entertaining that Rose White said to him...

ROSE WHITE: Please come visit us every evening and sit by our fire.

BEAR: Yes, I will come.

NARRATOR: The girls and their mother looked forward to the bear's visits each evening that winter. But at last, spring came, and the bear said...

BEAR: I must go away now. I have to guard my treasure from the wicked dwarf.

NARRATOR: Rose Red and Rose White were sad to see the bear go. They missed his nightly visits. One day that summer, Rose Red and Rose White were walking through the woods when they came upon a dwarf.

DWARF: What are you staring at, you silly girls? Help me get out of this!

ROSE RED: What's the matter?

DWARF: Are you blind? Can't you see that my beard is caught in this tree?

NARRATOR: Rose Red and Rose White pulled and pulled, but they could not get the ugly little man free. At last, Rose Red took her scissors out of her pocket and cut off the tip of his beard.

DWARF: You nasty girl! You cut my beautiful beard. May you be followed by bad luck!

NARRATOR: Then the dwarf stomped away, carrying a sack of gold that had been lying at the base of the tree. A few weeks later, Rose White and Rose Red were again walking in the forest when they heard someone screaming.

DWARF: Help! Help! Doggone this bird!!

ROSE WHITE: What's wrong, little man?

DWARF: Silly girl! Can't you see that this eagle has me in its claws? If I don't get away soon, he'll fly off with me!

NARRATOR: Rose Red and Rose White pulled on the dwarf, but they could not free him.

ROSE WHITE: Rose Red, you'll have to take out your scissors again and cut off some more of his beard.

ROSE RED: I guess you're right.

DWARF: You nasty girls! Look at my beautiful beard! You have ruined it!

NARRATOR: Then he picked up a sack of jewels and stomped off. A little white later, he stopped to count his jewels.

DWARF: ...five, six, seven, eight, nine, ten....Oh, how you glitter, my pretties!

NARRATOR: Rose Red and Rose White had not yet gone home. They were still walking in the woods when they came upon the dwarf once more.

DWARF: You horrid girls! Why are you spying on me? Be off with you, or I'll strike you dead!

NARRATOR: At these words, a great roar filled the forest. A huge bear came rushing out of the woods. He struck the dwarf a mighty blow with his paw, and the dwarf fell down dead. Rose Red and Rose White huddled together in terror.

BEAR: Don't be frightened, girls. Don't you recognize your old friend?

NARRATOR: Then slowly, the bear's fur began to fall away from him. He was no longer a bear, but a handsome prince. He had been under the dwarf's spell, but with the dwarf's death, the spell was broken. Rose Red became the prince's wife. Rose White and their mother came to live at the palace with the prince and Rose Red, and they all lived happily ever after.

Assembly Directions for Page 75
1. Color and cut out all pieces.
2. Paste roses onto front of crown, or string together on yarn to make a garland.
3. Trace crown pattern, color it, and cut it out. Use for prince.

Note: Use bear headband from page 71.

SLEEPING BEAUTY

NARRATOR:	Once upon a time, in a far-away kingdom, a baby girl was born to the king and queen.
KING:	I will give a great feast in honor of our new baby princess. I will invite all the nobles of my kingdom and all the fairies. But there are thirteen fairies in my kingdom. I cannot invite them all because I have only twelve golden plates. Oh well, I won't invite the Bad Fairy. Perhaps she will not care.
NARRATOR:	The day of the feast arrived, and all the people in the kingdom joined in the celebration. After the meal, the first eleven fairies each gave the young princess a gift. Suddenly, a blast of cold air swept through the palace.
BAD FAIRY:	So you did not think I was important enough to be invited to the feast? Ha! You fairies have each given the princess a gift. Now she will receive a gift from me! Hear this: when she turns sixteen, the princess will prick her finger on the needle of a spinning wheel and fall down dead!
NARRATOR:	With that, the Bad Fairy disappeared. The king and all of his friends wept when they heard the Bad Fairy's words. But then the twelfth fairy spoke.
TWELFTH FAIRY:	I have not yet given my gift. I cannot undo the Bad Fairy's gift, but I can soften it. The princess will not die, but she will fall into a deep sleep for one hundred years.
KING:	Oh, thank you, good fairy. I will also do what I can to stop the Bad Fairy's words from coming true. Now hear this. All the spinning wheels in the kingdom are to be burned.
NARRATOR:	So the young princess grew up, never knowing what a spinning wheel looked like. On her sixteenth birthday, she decided to explore the castle. She came to an old tower and climbed the stairs. At the top was a small room where an old woman sat spinning at her spinning wheel.
SLEEPING BEAUTY:	What are you doing, old woman?
OLD WOMAN:	I am spinning. Would you like to try it?
SLEEPING BEAUTY:	Oh yes, please. I would.
NARRATOR:	Now, the old woman was really the Bad Fairy in disguise. She let the princess sit down at her wheel to spin.
SLEEPING BEAUTY:	Ouch! I pricked my finger!
NARRATOR:	Instantly, the princess fell into a deep sleep. At the same time, all the animals and people in the castle also fell asleep. As the years passed, huge

NARRATOR (con't.): thorn bushes grew up around the castle until it could not be seen. From time to time, brave young men came to try and free the princess. But the thorns were magically strong, and no one could get through them.

After many long years had passed, a king's son rode into the kingdom. He had heard legends of a sleeping beauty in a castle hidden by thorns. The young prince set out to find the castle. But the hundred years were at an end.

PRINCE: This must be the castle. But what is this I see? These thorn bushes are turning into a garden of beautiful flowers, right before my very eyes!

NARRATOR: The flowers parted to let the prince through. He entered the courtyard.

PRINCE: Why, everyone here is asleep -- the king, the queen, even the animals! Hmmm. I wonder what is at the top of this tower. I think I'll climb the stairs and see.

NARRATOR: When he reached the top, the prince saw the sleeping princess.

PRINCE: What a beautiful princess. I must kiss her sweet lips!

NARRATOR: When the prince bent and kissed her, Sleeping Beauty opened her eyes and smiled up at him. As everyone in the castle awoke, Sleeping Beauty and the prince came down the tower stairs and stood before the king.

KING: Young man, you have broken the spell by kissing my daughter. You may have her hand in marriage.

NARRATOR: The prince and Sleeping Beauty were very happy. They had a glorious wedding, and everyone lived happily ever after.

Assembly Directions for Page 79
1. Color the castle, and cut it out.
2. Fold back castle sides on dotted lines.
3. Stand castle up.

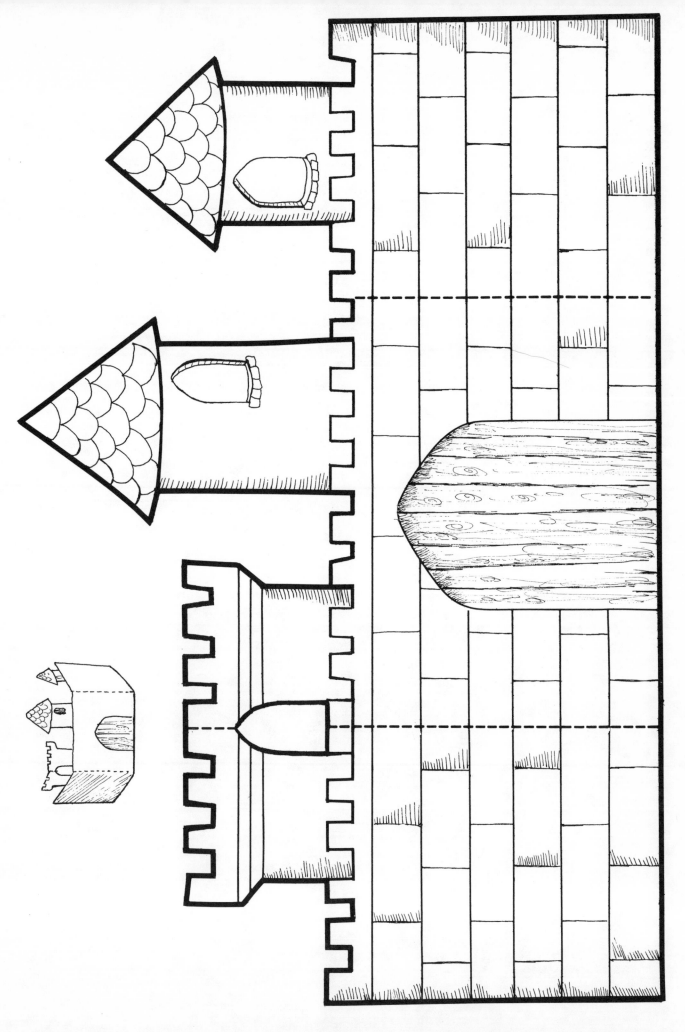

CINDERELLA

NARRATOR: Once upon a time, a girl lived with her step-mother and two step-sisters. They were very cruel to the girl, and made her work hard. She was given only rags to wear, so after her work was done, she would sit by the fireplace in the cinders and ashes to keep warm. Her wicked step-sisters teased her and called her "Cinderella."

One day, the prince of the land sent a messenger through the kingdom.

MESSENGER: Hear ye, hear he! The prince is giving a grand ball. All the young ladies in the kingdom are invited. Hear ye, hear ye!

STEP-SISTER #1: Oh, what fun! A ball! I must have the most beautiful dress at the ball. Cinderella, go fetch my blue gown. You must sew more lace around the neck.

STEP-SISTER #2: Cinderella, my pink dress must be hemmed. Go get it at once.

CINDERELLA: But when will I have time to get my dress ready for the ball?

STEP-SISTERS: Don't be silly, Cinderella. You can't go to the ball. What would you wear, your rags? Ha, ha, ha!

NARRATOR: The day of the ball arrived. The step-sisters dressed and were ready to go.

STEP-SISTER #1: Look at my lovely dress. I'm sure the prince will want to dance with me.

STEP-SISTER #2: Bye, bye, Cinderella. Have a nice time sitting in the cinders! Ha, ha, ha, ha!

NARRATOR: After her step-sisters left, Cinderella sat down and began to cry. Suddenly, a lovely fairy appeared.

CINDERELLA: Oh, my! Who are you?

FAIRY GODMOTHER: I am your fairy godmother. Now tell me, my dear, why are you crying?

CINDERELLA: I...I wanted to go to the prince's ball.

FAIRY GODMOTHER: And so you shall. Dry your tears, my child, and bring me a pumpkin.

NARRATOR: Cinderella found a huge orange pumpkin. Her fairy godmother waved her wand, and it turned into a golden coach.

FAIRY GODMOTHER: Now bring me six white mice.

NARRATOR: Cinderella did as she was told. With a wave of the wand, the mice were turned into six white horses to pull the coach.

FAIRY GODMOTHER: Now bring me a rat.

NARRATOR: When Cinderella brought the rat, her fairy godmother changed it into a footman to drive the coach. Finally, the fairy godmother waved her

NARRATOR (con't.): wand over Cinderella. Magically, her rags turned into the finest gown in the land. On her feet appeared dainty glass slippers.

FAIRY GODMOTHER: Now you are ready to go to the ball. But, remember! You must return by midnight, or all your finery will turn back into rags.

CINDERELLA: Oh, thank you, Fairy Godmother, thank you! And I will remember, I promise!

NARRATOR: When Cinderella arrived at the ball, her stepsisters did not recognize her in her fine clothes. The prince saw her come in and thought she was the most beautiful girl there. He rushed to her side and said...

PRINCE: Lovely lady, will you dance with me?

CINDERELLA: With pleasure, my prince.

NARRATOR: All evening, the prince danced only with Cinderella. She had such a wonderful time that she forgot her fairy godmother's warning until the clock began to strike midnight.

CINDERELLA: Oh no! I must go at once!

PRINCE: Wait! Wait! You haven't told me your name!

NARRATOR: But Cinderella ran out of the ballroom and down the stairs. She lost one of her glass slippers, but she did not have time to stop for it. The prince, who was following her, stopped to pick it up.

PRINCE: I will try this slipper on every lady in the land, and marry the one it fits!

NARRATOR: The next day, the prince set out to find the owner of the slipper. Many girls tried it on, but none could fit into it. At last, the prince reached Cinderella's house. Both of her step-sisters tried and tried to squeeze into the tiny slipper, but failed. As the prince turned to leave, Cinderella said...

CINDERELLA: May I please try on the slipper?

PRINCE: Yes, of course! Here, try it. Why, it fits perfectly! You were the girl at the ball! Come, we will be married at once!

NARRATOR: The prince took Cinderella away with him to the castle. There was a great wedding, and Cinderella and her prince lived happily ever after.

Assembly Directions for Page 83

1. Color and cut out all pieces.
2. Punch holes as marked.
3. Use paper fasteners to attach arms and head to body.

THE THREE BILLY GOATS GRUFF

NARRATOR: Once there were three billy goat brothers, and their last name was Gruff. They lived together on a green slope next to the river. One day, Big Billy Goat Gruff looked across the river and said...

BIG BILLY GOAT GRUFF: The grass on that hillside is greener than ours. Let's go eat that grass over there and make ourselves fat.

NARRATOR: In order to get to the hillside, the Billy Goats Gruff had to cross a bridge. Under the bridge, there lived an ugly troll with eyes as big as saucers and a nose as long as a poker.

Little Billy Goat Gruff was the first to cross the bridge.

(SOUND EFFECTS: Tip, tap, tip, tap.)

TROLL: Who's that tramping over my bridge?

LITTLE BILLY GOAT GRUFF: It is I, Little Billy Goat Gruff. I'm going across to the hillside to eat the grass and make myself fat.

TROLL: Get off my bridge, or I'll come up and eat you!

LITTLE BILLY GOAT GRUFF: Oh, you wouldn't like me. I'm too skinny. Wait until Middle-Sized Billy Goat Gruff comes along. He's fatter than I. He'll make a better meal for you, I'm sure.

TROLL: Well, all right. Be off with you then.

NARRATOR: A little while later, Middle-Sized Billy Goat Gruff came across the bridge.

(SOUND EFFECTS: Trip, Trap, Trip, Trap.)

TROLL: Who's that tramping over my bridge?

MIDDLE-SIZED
   BILLY GOAT GRUFF: It is I, Middle-Sized Billy Goat Gruff. I am going across to the hillside to eat the grass and make myself fat.

TROLL: Get off my bridge, or I'll come up and eat you!

MIDDLE-SIZED
   BILLY GOAT GRUFF: Why don't you wait for my big brother, Big Billy Goat Gruff? He's fatter than I am, and he'll make a much better meal for you, I'm sure.

TROLL: Well, all right. Be off with you then.

NARRATOR: Soon, Big Billy Goat Gruff came across the bridge.

(SOUND EFFECTS: TRIP, TRAP, TRIP, TRAP.)

TROLL: Who's that tramping over my bridge?

BIG BILLY GOAT GRUFF: It is I, Big Billy Goat Gruff. I'm going across to the hillside to eat the grass and make myself fat.

TROLL: Oh no, you're not! I'm coming to gobble you up!

BIG BILLY GOAT GRUFF: Come on, then! I've got two long spears, and with them I'll poke your eyeballs out your ears. I've got two curling stones, and I'll crush you to bits, both body and bones!

TROLL: We'll see about that! Get off my bridge, or I'll eat you!

NARRATOR: With that, the troll jumped up onto the bridge. Big Billy Goat Bruff lowered his horns and ran at the troll. He caught the troll on his horns and tossed him SPLASH! into the river. Then he walked across to the hillside to join his brothers. Big Billy Goat Gruff and his brothers ate so much grass and got so fat that they were barely able to walk home. And, if the fat hasn't fallen off of them, they are still fat and living happily ever after!

Assembly Directions for Page 87
1. Color bridge scene and cut out.
2. Color figures and cut out.
3. Cut out finger loops. Fold flaps and paste one to the back of each figure, leaving space for finger.

FOLD FLAP & PASTE | FINGER LOOP | FOLD FLAP & PASTE

FOLD FLAP AND PASTE | FINGER LOOP | FOLD FLAP & PASTE

FOLD FLAP AND PASTE | FINGER LOOP | FOLD FLAP AND PASTE

FOLD FLAP AND PASTE | FINGER LOOP | FOLD FLAP AND PASTE

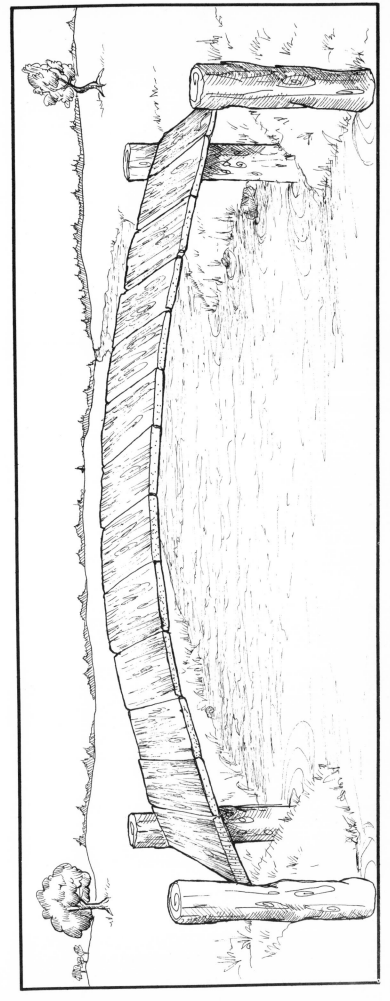

THE GINGERBREAD MAN

NARRATOR: Once upon a time, a little old woman and a little old man lived together in a little old house. Their children were all grown up and gone, and they were very lonely. One day, the little old woman decided to bake some gingerbread. She mixed up the batter in a bowl. Then she rolled out the dough, and cut it out in the shape of a gingerbread man. Soon, the gingergread man was ready to be put in the oven. While the gingerbread man was baking, the little old woman thought and thought about him. She loved the gingerbread man with all her heart. Maybe it was her love for him that made a strange thing happen. For when the old woman opened the oven to take the gingerbread man out, he jumped to the floor all by himself and ran out the kitchen door.

OLD WOMAN: Stop! Stop!

GINGERBREAD MAN: Run, run, as fast as you can. You can't catch me, I'm the Gingerbread Man!

NARRATOR: The old woman started to chase the Gingerbread Man, but he soon left her far behind. As he ran down the road, he passed a farmer.

FARMER: Stop! Stop! I want to eat you!

GINGERBREAD MAN: Run, run, as fast as you can. You can't catch me, I'm the Gingerbread Man! I ran away from the old woman, and I can run away from you, I can!

NARRATOR: The farmer tried to catch the Gingerbread Man, but he couldn't stop him. Soon, the Gingerbread Man ran past a cow.

COW: Stop! Stop! I want to eat you!

GINGERBREAD MAN: Run, run, as fast as you can. You can't catch me, I'm the Gingerbread Man. I ran away from the old woman and a farmer, and I can run away from you, I can!

NARRATOR: The cow tried to catch the Gingerbread Man, but she couldn't stop him. Soon, the Gingerbread Man ran past a pig.

PIG: Stop! Stop! I want to eat you!

GINGERBREAD MAN: Run, run, as fast as you can. You can't catch me, I'm the Gingerbread Man. I ran away from the old woman, the farmer, and the cow, and I can run away from you, I can!

NARRATOR: The pig tried to catch the Gingerbread Man, but he couldn't stop him. Soon, the Gingerbread Man ran past a fox.

FOX: Well, well, Gingerbread Man. Why do you run so fast on such a hot day?

GINGERBREAD MAN: An old woman, a farmer, a cow, and a pig are trying to catch me. They all want to eat me!

FOX: They do? Well, I'll help you get away from them. You keep running, and I'll run along beside you.

NARRATOR: The Gingerbread Man was happy to find a friend. So away he ran with the fox at his side. Before long, they came to a wide river.

GINGERBREAD MAN: What should I do now? I can't swim!

FOX: Don't worry. I'll carry you across the river. Hop on my tail.

NARRATOR: So the Gingerbread Man jumped on the fox's tail, and they began to cross the river. Soon, the fox said...

FOX: The river is getting deeper. Hop on my shoulder, or you'll get wet.

NARRATOR: So the Gingerbread Man jumped onto the fox's shoulder, and on they went.

FOX: The river is getting deeper. Hop on my nose so you won't get wet.

NARRATOR: So the Gingerbread Man jumped on the fox's nose. The fox opened his mouth wide, and SNAP! SNAP! That was the end of the Gingerbread Man!

Assembly Directions for Page 91
1. Color all puzzle pieces.
2. Paste page to a sheet of drawing paper.
3. Cut out all pieces.
4. Assemble the puzzle.

91

The REAL Happily Ever After Game Instructions

Assembly Directions for Pages 93 and 95

1. Color game board as desired.
2. Tear out game board and paste inside a manila folder.
3. Cut out pointer. Back it with heavy paper and attach to circle in game board with paper fastener.
4. Color beans and cut them out. Store them in an envelope inside the folder.
5. Cut out the directions at the bottom of this page. Paste them inside the folder across from the game board.

Variations

1. Replace the terms "character," "setting," and "prop" with "person," "place," and "thing."

2. Make this an individual activity. Write "prop," "character," and "setting" on spring-type clothespins (one for each board picture). Direct student to clip clothespins onto the correct pictures. Make the activity self-checking by writing correct answers on the outside of the folder.

The REAL
Happily Ever After Game
Directions

1. Choose a magic bean from the envelope for your marker.
2. Place all markers on "Start."
3. The first player spins and moves his/her marker to the first space on the board having a correct answer. (For example, if the pointer stops at "character," the player places the bean on the picture of Jack.)
4. If a player moves to an incorrect space, he/she must return the bean to where it was at the beginning of that move.
5. Players take turns spinning and moving beans to continue the game.
6. The first player to land on the beanstalk by an exact spin wins the game.

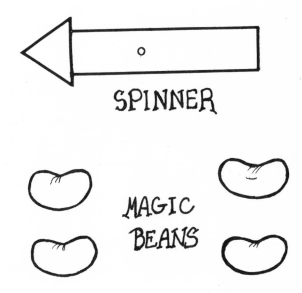

SPINNER

MAGIC BEANS

THE REAL HAPPILY EVER AFTER GAME!

GINGER BREAD / HOUSE

LITTLE MERMAID

DWARF

WOODS

APPLE / POISONED

GLASS SLIPPER

BEAST

CASTLE

TOWER

BIG BAD WOLF

POT

PORRIDGE

GINGERBREAD BOY

SNOW WHITE

HOUSE OF STRAW

JACK / JACK

START

BEANSTALK

MAGIC WAND / MAGIC WAND

CHARACTER — SETTING — PROP — CHARACTER — SETTING — PROP